POKÉMON

GREATEST BATTLES

By Maria Barbo

W9-CBU-552

SCHOLASTIC INC.

New York   Toronto   London   Auckland   Sydney
Mexico City   New Delhi   Hong Kong   Buenos Aires

ISBN 0-439-68673-3

12 11 10 9 8 7 6 5 4 3 2   4 5 6 7 8/0

Printed in the U.S.A.
First printing, September 2004

Pokémon fans, get ready for . . .
Fantastic face-offs!
Magnificent match-ups!
And the best Pokémon battles ever!

Have you ever wanted to see Pikachu face off against Meowth?

How about Ash's Pokémon in a head-to-head battle against Team Rocket . . .
or even Team Magma?!

Now is your chance! In this book, you will find your favorite Pokémon in the biggest
and best Pokémon battles ever seen! And YOU get to decide who wins and who loses.

How do you know who will win?

Check out the stats.

See how your favorite Pokémon match up!

Who's faster?

Who's bigger?

Who's stronger?

Who has the best defense?

Who has the strongest attack?

Who has the coolest ability?

Who will win?

And who will lose?

NOW, YOU GET
TO CHOOSE!

MY POKÉMON IS BETTER THAN YOUR POKÉMON!

WELL, HOW DO YOU KNOW?

You can never know for sure who will win a Pokémon face-off—until it's over! But you can make a good guess.

Here are THREE things to help you make your best guess:

1) TYPE

A Pokémon's Type is the most important part of choosing who will win a Pokémon battle.

Check out the next page for the inside scoop on understanding TYPE.

2) EXPERIENCE AND SKILL

Some Pokémon are faster than others. Some Pokémon are stronger. Some have been in more competitions. And some have evolved while others have not. All of these things play a role in which Pokémon will win a match-up.

3) PERSONALITY

Personality is what makes every Pokémon special. And it plays a part in who will win a battle. Some Pokémon are bold and brave. They like to fight. Other Pokémon are sweet, shy, or easily frightened. Some Pokémon are happy, and others get lonely.

Ash's Pikachu is a great example. You may not think this little Electric Pokémon stands a chance against a powerful Pokémon like Mewtwo, but Pikachu has a lot of spirit. It never gives up and it does NOT like to lose. When Pikachu faced Mewtwo, Pikachu won the battle!

REMEMBER:
You can make a good guess, but you won't know who the winner is until the match is over.

TIPS ON TYPE

Every Pokémon has a TYPE, like Water, Fire, Ground, or Poison. Type tells you what kinds of moves your Pokémon will use in battle. For example, Water Pokémon use moves like Splash and Whirlpool. While Electric Pokémon use skills like Thunder and Spark.

There are SEVENTEEN basic Types. Each Type does better against some Pokémon than others.

For example, in a battle between a Water Pokémon and a Fire Pokémon, the Water Pokémon has a better chance of winning. That's because water puts out fire. But Fire Pokémon are more likely to beat Ice Pokémon because Fire melts Ice. It doesn't mean Water will ALWAYS beat Fire, but Water has the advantage (has a better chance to win). It's like a super-charged game of Rock, Paper, Scissors.

DOUBLE TROUBLE

Pokémon can have more than one Type. Blaziken is a Fire and Fighting Type. That means it has twice both Fire and a Fighting skills. Blaziken is double the trouble and double the fun!

TYPE CHART

NORMAL

Best Against: —

Worst Against: Rock and Steel Types

Most Likely to Tie With: Ghost Type

GRASS

Best Against: Water, Ground, and Rock Types

Worst Against: Fire, Grass, Poison, Flying, Bug, Dragon, and Steel Types

FIRE

Best Against: Grass, Ice, Bug, and Steel Types

Worst Against: Fire, Water, Rock, and Dragon Types

ICE

Best Against: Grass, Ground, Flying, and Dragon Types

Worst Against: Fire, Water, Ice, and Steel Types

WATER

Best Against: Fire, Ground, and Rock Types.

Worst Against: Water, Grass, and Dragon Types

FIGHTING

Best Against: Normal, Ice, Rock, Dark, and Steel Types

Worst Against: Poison, Flying, Psychic, and Bug Types

Most Likely to Tie With: Ghost Type

ELECTRIC

Best Against: Water and Flying Types

Worst Against: Electric, Grass, and Dragon Types

POISON

Best Against: Grass Type

Worst Against: Poison, Ground, Rock, and Ghost Types

Most Likely to Tie With: Steel Type

GROUND

Best Against: Fire, Electric, Poison, Rock, and Steel Types

Worst Against: Grass and Bug Types

Most Likely to Tie With: Flying Type

FLYING

Best Against: Grass, Fighting, and Bug Types

Worst Against: Electric, Rock, and Steel Types

PSYCHIC

Best Against: Fighting and Poison Types

Worst Against: Psychic and Steel Types

Most Likely to Tie With: Dark Type

BUG

Best Against: Grass, Psychic, and Dark Types

Worst Against: Fire, Fighting, Poison, Flying, Ghost, and Steel Types

ROCK

Best Against: Fire, Ice, Flying, and Bug Types

Worst Against: Fighting, Ground, and Steel Types

GHOST

Best Against: Psychic and Ghost Types

Worst Against: Dark and Steel Types

Most Likely to Tie With: Normal Type

DRAGON

Best Against: Dragon Types

Worst Against: Steel Types

DARK

Best Against: Psychic and Ghost Types

Worst Against: Fighting, Steel, and Dark Types

STEEL

Best Against: Ice and Rock Types

Worst Against: Fire, Water, Electric, and Steel Types

NOW, TURN THE PAGE FOR THE GREATEST POKéMON MATCH-UPS EVER. LET THE BATTLES BEGIN!

ASH'S TREECKO™

Type: Grass   **Height: 1' 8"**   **Weight: 11 lbs**   **Ability: Overgrow**

HP

Speed

Attack

Defense

SP Attack

SP Defense

Treecko   **Grovyle**   **Sceptile**

Who do you think will win? 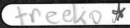 *treeko* ✶

| Type: Rock & Grass | Height: 3' 3" | Weight: 52 lbs | Ability: Suction Cups |

treeko

HP	
Speed	
Attack	
Defense	
SP Attack	
SP Defense	

Lileep **Cradily**

GROVYLE™

Type: Grass	Height: 2' 11"	Weight: 48 lbs	Ability: Overgrow

HP
Speed
Attack
Defense
SP Attack
SP Defense

Treecko › **Grovyle** › **Sceptile**

Who do you think will win? *grovyle*

Type: Water	Height: 1' 4"	Weight: 19 lbs	Ability: Thick Fat & Huge Power

HP
Speed
Attack
Defense
SP Attack
SP Defense

Azurill ❯ **Marill** ❯ **Azumarill**

SCEPTILE™

Type: Grass   **Height:** 5' 7"   **Weight:** 17 lbs   **Ability:** Overgrow

HP
Speed
Attack
Defense
SP Attack
SP Defense

Treecko > **Grovyle** > **Sceptile**

VS. GRAUELER™

Who do you think will win? sceptile

Type: Rock & Ground   **Height:** 3' 3"   **Weight:** 232 lbs   **Ability:** Rack Head & Sturdy

HP	
Speed	
Attack	
Defense	
SP Attack	
SP Defense	

Geodude ⟩ **Graveler** ⟩ **Golem**

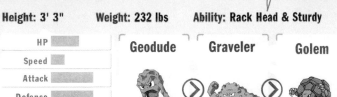

13

MUDKIP™

Type: Water   **Height: 1' 4"**   **Weight: 17 lbs**   **Ability: Torrent**

HP
Speed
Attack
Defense
SP Attack
SP Defense

Mudkip > **Marshtomp** > **Swampert**

VS. ZIGZAGOON™

Who do you think will win? Mudkip

Type: Normal	**Height: 1' 4"**	**Weight: 39 lbs**	**Ability: Pickup**

- HP
- Speed
- Attack
- Defense
- SP Attack
- SP Defense

Zigzagoon > **Linoone**

MARSHTOMP™

Type: Water & Ground   **Height: 2' 4"**   **Weight: 62 lbs**   **Ability: Torrent**

- HP
- Speed
- Attack
- Defense
- SP Attack
- SP Defense

Mudkip  › **Marshtomp**  › **Swampert**

Who do you think will win? swampert

Type: **Bug & Water**   Height: **1' 8"**   Weight: **4 lbs**   Ability: **Swift Swim**

HP
Speed
Attack
Defense
SP Attack
SP Defense

Surskit › **Masquerain**

cute

SWAMPERT™

| Type: Water & Ground | Height: 4' 11" | Weight: 118 lbs | Ability: Torrent |

HP
Speed
Attack
Defense
SP Attack
SP Defense

Mudkip > **Marshtomp** > **Swampert**

Who do you think will win? swampert

Type: Fire & Rock   **Height:** 2' 7"   **Weight:** 121 lbs   **Ability:** Magma Armor & Flame Body

HP
Speed
Attack
Defense
SP Attack
SP Defense

Slugma ❯ **Magcargo**

MAY'S TORCHIC™

Type: Fire	Height: 1' 4"	Weight: 6 lbs	Ability: Blaze

HP	
Speed	
Attack	
Defense	
SP Attack	
SP Defense	

Torchic ➤ **Combusken** ➤ **Blaziken**

VS. SHROOMISH™

Who do you think will win?  torchic

Type: Grass	Height: 1' 4"	Weight: 10 lbs	Ability: Effect Spore

HP	
Speed	
Attack	
Defense	
SP Attack	
SP Defense	

 Shroomish Breloom

COMBUSKEN ™

Type: Fire & Fighting	Height: 2' 11"	Weight: 43 lbs	Ability: Blaze

- HP
- Speed
- Attack
- Defense
- SP Attack
- SP Defense

Torchic  **Combusken**  **Blaziken**

VS. MIGHTYENA ™

Who do you think will win? Mightyena

Type: Dark   **Height: 3' 3"**   **Weight: 82 lbs**   **Ability: Intimidate**

| HP |
| Speed |
| Attack |
| Defense |
| SP Attack |
| SP Defense |

Poochyena 〉 Mightyena

23

BLAZIKEN ™

Type: Fire & Fighting   **Height:** 6' 3"   **Weight:** 115 lbs   **Ability:** Blaze

HP	
Speed	
Attack	
Defense	
SP Attack	
SP Defense	

Torchic **Combusken** **Blaziken**

VS. SHARPEDO™

Who do you think will win? Blaziken

Type: Water & Dark **Height: 5' 11"** **Weight: 196 lbs** **Ability: Rough Skin**

HP	
Speed	
Attack	
Defense	
SP Attack	
SP Defense	

Carvanha **Sharpedo**

THE PICHU BROS.™

Type: Electric **Height:** 1' 0" **Weight:** 4 lbs **Ability:** Static

HP	
Speed	
Attack	
Defense	
SP Attack	
SP Defense	

Pichu > **Pikachu** > **Raichu**

VS. PLUSLE AND MINUN ™

Who do you think will win? Plusle & Minun

| Type: Electric | Height: 1' 4" | Weight: 9 lbs | Ability: Plus |
| Type: Electric | Height: 1' 4" | Weight: 9 lbs | Ability: Minus |

HP

Speed

Attack

Defense

SP Attack

SP Defense

Does not evolve

PIKACHU™

Type: Electric Height: 1' 4" Weight: 13 lbs Ability: Static

HP	
Speed	
Attack	
Defense	
SP Attack	
SP Defense	

Pichu ❯ Pikachu ❯ Raichu

Who do you think will win? pikacho

Type: Rock   **Height: 3' 3"**   **Weight: 214 lbs**   **Ability: Sturdy & Magnet**

HP
Speed
Attack
Defense
SP Attack
SP Defense

Does not evolve

RAICHU™

Type: Electric	Height: 2' 7"	Weight: 66 lbs	Ability: Static

HP
Speed
Attack
Defense
SP Attack
SP Defense

Pichu > Pikachu > Raichu

VS. SHIFTRY™

Who do you think will win? RAichu

Type: Grass & Dark   **Height:** 4' 3"   **Weight:** 131 lbs   **Ability:** Chlorophyll & Early Bird

HP
Speed
Attack
Defense
SP Attack
SP Defense

Seedot → **Nuzleaf** → **Shiftry**

ASH'S CORPHISH™

Type: Water	Height: 2' 0"	Weight: 25 lbs	Ability: Hyper Cutter & Shell Armor

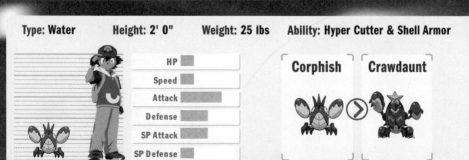

HP
Speed
Attack
Defense
SP Attack
SP Defense

Corphish Crawdaunt

VS. TEAM ROCKET'S CACNEA™

Who do you think will win? corfish

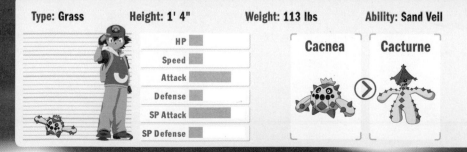

Type: Grass   **Height:** 1' 4"   **Weight:** 113 lbs   **Ability:** Sand Veil

HP
Speed
Attack
Defense
SP Attack
SP Defense

Cacnea > **Cacturne**

ASH'S TAILLOW™

Type: Normal & Flying   **Height: 1' 0"**   **Weight: 5 lbs**   **Ability: Guts**

HP	
Speed	
Attack	
Defense	
SP Attack	
SP Defense	

Taillow ❯ **Swellow**

VS. MAY'S WURMPLE™

Who do you think will win? *tailow* ~~~

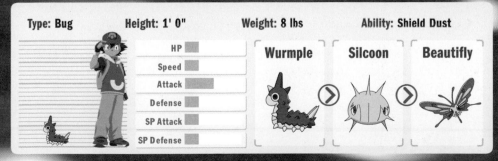

Type: Bug   **Height: 1' 0"**   **Weight: 8 lbs**   **Ability: Shield Dust**

HP	
Speed	
Attack	
Defense	
SP Attack	
SP Defense	

Wurmple → **Silcoon** → **Beautifly**

POOCHYENA™

Type: Dark	Height: 1' 8"	Weight: 90 lbs	Ability: Run Away

HP	
Speed	
Attack	
Defense	
SP Attack	
SP Defense	

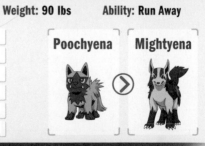

Poochyena ❯ Mightyena

VS. BELDUM™

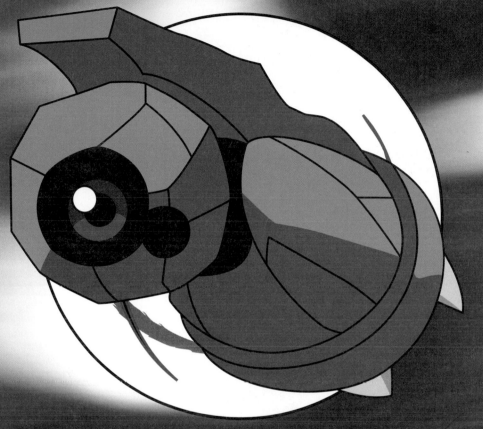

Who do you think will win?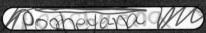

Pomegarai (handwritten)

Type: Steel & Psychic   **Height:** 2' 0"   **Weight:** 210 lbs   **Ability:** Clear Body

HP
Speed
Attack
Defense
SP Attack
SP Defense

Beldum ❯ **Metang** ❯ **Metagross**

TEAM ROCKET'S WOBBUFFET™

Type: Psychic	Height: 4' 3"	Weight: 63 lbs	Ability: Shadow Tag

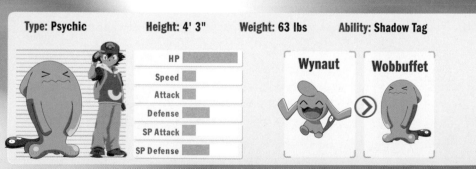

HP
Speed
Attack
Defense
SP Attack
SP Defense

Wynaut > Wobbuffet

VS. SWALOT ™

Who do you think will win?

Type: Poison **Height: 5' 7"** **Weight: 176 lbs** **Ability: Liquid Ooze & Sticky Hold**

HP	
Speed	
Attack	
Defense	
SP Attack	
SP Defense	

Gulpin ❯ **Swalot**

WYNAUT ™

Type: Psychic	Height: 2' 0"	Weight: 31 lbs	Ability: Shadow Tag

HP
Speed
Attack
Defense
SP Attack
SP Defense

Wynaut › **Wobbuffet**

VS. ARON™

Who do you think will win? Aron

Type: Steel & Rock **Height:** 1' 4" **Weight:** 132 lbs **Ability:** Sturdy & Rock Head

HP	
Speed	
Attack	
Defense	
SP Attack	
SP Defense	

Aron ❯ **Lairon** ❯ **Aggron**

ASH'S PIKACHU™

Type: Electric   **Height:** 1' 4"   **Weight:** 13 lbs   **Ability:** Static

HP	
Speed	
Attack	
Defense	
SP Attack	
SP Defense	

Pichu > **Pikachu** > **Raichu**

Who do you think will win? 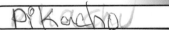 Pikachu

Type: Water & Flying **Height: 3' 11"** **Weight: 62 lbs** **Ability: Keen Eye**

HP
Speed
Attack
Defense
SP Attack
SP Defense

Wingull 〉 **Pelipper**

ASH'S PIKACHU™

Type: Electric	Height: 1' 4"	Weight: 13 lbs	Ability: Static

HP
Speed
Attack
Defense
SP Attack
SP Defense

Pichu > **Pikachu** > **Raichu**

Who do you think will win? Pikachu

Type: Normal   **Height: 4' 7"**   **Weight: 103 lbs**   **Ability: Vital Spirit**

HP
Speed
Attack
Defense
SP Attack
SP Defense

Slakoth   **Vigoroth**   **Slaking**

ASH'S PIKACHU™

Type: Electric   **Height:** 1' 4"   **Weight:** 13 lbs   **Ability:** Static

HP	
Speed	
Attack	
Defense	
SP Attack	
SP Defense	

Pichu > **Pikachu** > **Raichu**

VS. GEODUDE ™

Who do you think will win? *pikachu*

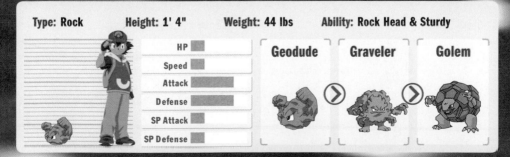

Type: Rock **Height: 1' 4"** **Weight: 44 lbs** **Ability: Rock Head & Sturdy**

HP
Speed
Attack
Defense
SP Attack
SP Defense

Geodude → **Graveler** → **Golem**

ASH'S PIKACHU™

| Type: Electric | Height: 1' 4" | Weight: 13 lbs | Ability: Static |

HP
Speed
Attack
Defense
SP Attack
SP Defense

Pichu > **Pikachu** > **Raichu**

VS. TEAM ROCKET'S MEOWTH™

Who do you think will win? Pikachu

| Type: Normal | Height: 1' 4" | Weight: 9 lbs | Ability: Scratch |

HP
Speed
Attack
Defense
SP Attack
SP Defense

Meowth > Persian

DUSKULL™

Type: Ghost	Height: 2' 7"	Weight: 33 lbs	Ability: Levitate

HP
Speed
Attack
Defense
SP Attack
SP Defense

Duskull > **Dusclops**

Who do you think will win? *Duskull*

Type: Poison & Flying   **Height: 2' 7"**   **Weight: 17 lbs**   **Ability: Inner Focus**

HP
Speed
Attack
Defense
SP Attack
SP Defense

Zubat > Golbat > Crobat

SHEDINJA ™

Type: Bug & Ghost   **Height: 2' 7"**   **Weight: 3 lbs**   **Ability: Wonder Guard**

HP	
Speed	
Attack	
Defense	
SP Attack	
SP Defense	

Ninjask ❯ **Nincada** ❯ **Shedinja**

Who do you think will win? shedinja

Type: Dark & Ghost   **Height: 1' 8"**   **Weight: 24 lbs**   **Ability: Keen Eye**

HP	
Speed	
Attack	
Defense	
SP Attack	
SP Defense	

**Does
not
evolve**

SEVIPER™

Type: Poison	Height: 8' 10"	Weight: 116 lbs	Ability: Shed Skin

HP	
Speed	
Attack	
Defense	
SP Attack	
SP Defense	

**Does
not
evolve**

VS. REGIROCK ™

Who do you think will win? seviper regirock

Type: Rock	Height: 5' 7"	Weight: 507 lbs	Ability: Clear Body

HP
Speed
Attack
Defense
SP Attack
SP Defense

Regirock > **Regice** > **Registeel**

BEAUTIFLY™

Type: Bug & Flying   **Height:** 3' 3"   **Weight:** 63 lbs   **Ability:** Swarm

HP
Speed
Attack
Defense
SP Attack
SP Defense

Wurmple ❯ **Silcoon** ❯ **Beautifly**

Who do you think will win? _Beautifly_

Type: Bug & Poison	Height: 3' 11"	Weight: 70 lbs	Ability: Shield Dust

HP	
Speed	
Attack	
Defense	
SP Attack	
SP Defense	

Wurmple > **Silcoon** > **Dustox**

SKITTY ™

Type: Normal	Height: 2' 0"	Weight: 24 lbs	Ability: Cute Charm

HP
Speed
Attack
Defense
SP Attack
SP Defense

Skitty

>

Delcatty

VS. LOUDRED ™

Who do you think will win? Skitty

Type: Normal **Height: 3' 3"** **Weight: 89 lbs** **Ability: Soundproof**

HP
Speed
Attack
Defense
SP Attack
SP Defense

Whismur	Loudred	Exploud

Type: Psychic	Height: 2' 4"	Weight: 67 lbs	Ability: Thick Fat & Own Tempo

HP
Speed
Attack
Defense
SP Attack
SP Defense

Spoink  > **Grumpig**

VS. IGGLYBUFF™

Who do you think will win? none

Type: Normal	Height: 1' 0"	Weight: 2 lbs	Ability: Cute Charm

HP
Speed
Attack
Defense
SP Attack
SP Defense

igglybuff > **Jigglypuff** > **WIgglytuff**

WALREIN ™

Type: Ice & Water	Height: 4' 7"	Weight: 332 lbs	Ability: Thick Fat

HP
Speed
Attack
Defense
SP Attack
SP Defense

Spheal ❯ **Sealeo** ❯ **Walrein**

VS. TORKOAL™

Who do you think will win? Walrien

Type: Fire   Height: 1' 8"   Weight: 177 lbs   Ability: White Smoke

HP
Speed
Attack
Defense
SP Attack
SP Defense

Does not evolve

TENTACRUEL ™

Type: Water & Poison **Height: 5' 3"** **Weight: 121 lbs** **Ability: Clear Body & Liquid Ooze**

HP	
Speed	
Attack	
Defense	
SP Attack	
SP Defense	

Tentacool 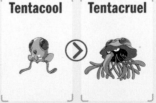 **Tentacruel**

Who do you think will win? Pentacruzi

Type: **Fighting**　　　Height: **3' 3"**　　　Weight: **191 lbs**　　　Ability: **Thick Fat & Guts**

HP	
Speed	
Attack	
Defense	
SP Attack	
SP Defense	

Makuhita　　　**Hariyama**

CACTURNE™

Type: Grass & Dark   **Height: 4' 3"**   **Weight: 171 lbs**   **Ability: Sand Veil**

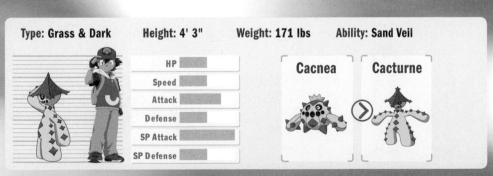

HP
Speed
Attack
Defense
SP Attack
SP Defense

Cacnea > Cacturne

VS. CRAWDAUNT ™

Who do you think will win? CRAWDAUNT

Type: Water & Dark   **Height:** 3' 7"   **Weight:** 72 lbs   **Ability:** Hyper Cutter & Shell Armor

HP
Speed
Attack
Defense
SP Attack
SP Defense

Corphish ❯ Crawdaunt

RAYQUAZA™

Type: Dragon & Flying	Height: 23' 0"	Weight: 455 lbs	Ability: Air Lock

HP

Speed

Attack

Defense

SP Attack

SP Defense

**Does
not
evolve**

VS. GYARADOS™

Who do you think will win? **Rayquaza**

Type: **Water & Flying**   Height: **21' 4"**   Weight: **518 lbs**   Ability: **Intimidate**

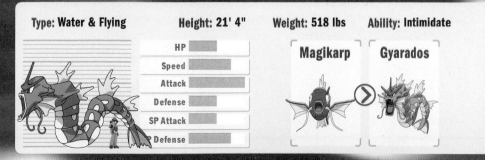

HP	
Speed	
Attack	
Defense	
SP Attack	
SP Defense	

Magikarp ❯ **Gyarados**

VENUSAUR™

| Type: Grass & Poison | Height: 6' 7" | Weight: 221 lbs | Ability: |

HP

Speed

Attack

Defense

SP Attack

SP Defense

Bulbasaur

Ivysaur

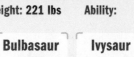

Venusaur

seceptile

Type: Grass	Height: 2' 11"	Weight: 48 lbs	Ability: Overgrow

HP
Speed
Attack
Defense
SP Attack
SP Defense

Treecko	Grovyle	Sceptile

CHARIZARD™

Type: Fire & Flying   **Height: 5' 7"**   **Weight: 200 lbs**   **Ability: Levitate**

HP	
Speed	
Attack	
Defense	
SP Attack	
SP Defense	

Charmander  ⟩ **Charmeleon** ⟩ **Charizard**

VS. BLAZIKEN™

Who do you think will win? Blaziken

Type: Fire & Fighting	Height: 6' 3"	Weight: 115 lbs	Ability: Blaze

		Torchic	Combusken	Blaziken
HP				
Speed				
Attack				
Defense				
SP Attack				
SP Defense				

GROUDON™

Type: Ground **Height: 11' 6"** **Weight: 2095 lbs** **Ability: Drought**

HP	
Speed	
Attack	
Defense	
SP Attack	
SP Defense	

**Does
not
evolve**

VS. HYOGRE™

Who do you think will win? *Hyogre*

Type: Water   Height: 14' 9"   Weight: 776 lbs   Ability: Drizzle

- HP
- Speed
- Attack
- Defense
- SP Attack
- SP Defense

Does not evolve

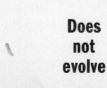

TM

Draw your favorite Pokémon here!

Type: Height: Weight: Ability:

HP

Speed

Attack

Defense

SP Attack

SP Defense

VS.

^{TM}

Draw your favorite Pokémon here!

Who do you think will win?

Type:　　　　　Height:　　　　　Weight:　　　　　Ability:

HP

Speed

Attack

Defense

SP Attack

SP Defense

™

Draw your favorite Pokémon here!

Type:	Height:	Weight:	Ability:

	HP
	Speed
	Attack
	Defense
	SP Attack
	SP Defense

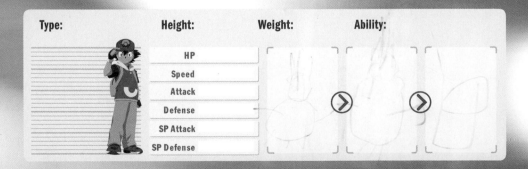

Draw your favorite Pokémon here!

Who do you think will win?

Type:

Height:

Weight:

Ability:

HP

Speed

Attack

Defense

SP Attack

SP Defense

NOW YOU ARE A POKÉMON MASTER!

CATCH YA LATER!